W9-CTI-039

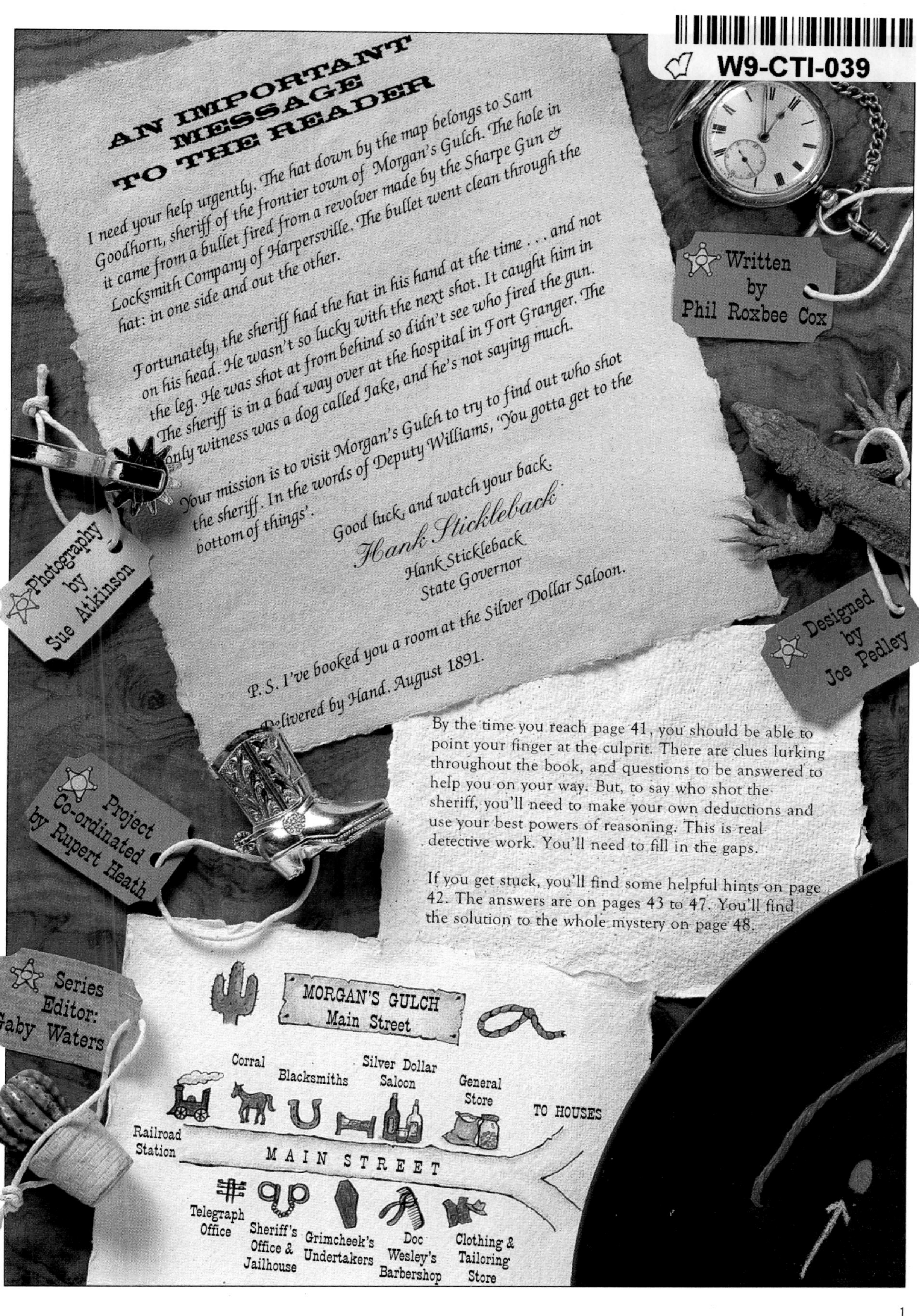

AN IMPORTANT MESSAGE TO THE READER

I need your help urgently. The hat down by the map belongs to Sam Goodhorn, sheriff of the frontier town of Morgan's Gulch. The hole in it came from a bullet fired from a revolver made by the Sharpe Gun & Locksmith Company of Harpersville. The bullet went clean through the hat: in one side and out the other.

Fortunately, the sheriff had the hat in his hand at the time . . . and not on his head. He wasn't so lucky with the next shot. It caught him in the leg. He was shot at from behind so didn't see who fired the gun. The sheriff is in a bad way over at the hospital in Fort Granger. The only witness was a dog called Jake, and he's not saying much.

Your mission is to visit Morgan's Gulch to try to find out who shot the sheriff. In the words of Deputy Williams, 'You gotta get to the bottom of things'.

Good luck, and watch your back.

Hank Stickleback

Hank Stickleback
State Governor

P. S. I've booked you a room at the Silver Dollar Saloon.

Delivered by Hand. August 1891.

By the time you reach page 41, you should be able to point your finger at the culprit. There are clues lurking throughout the book, and questions to be answered to help you on your way. But, to say who shot the sheriff, you'll need to make your own deductions and use your best powers of reasoning. This is real detective work. You'll need to fill in the gaps.

If you get stuck, you'll find some helpful hints on page 42. The answers are on pages 43 to 47. You'll find the solution to the whole mystery on page 48.

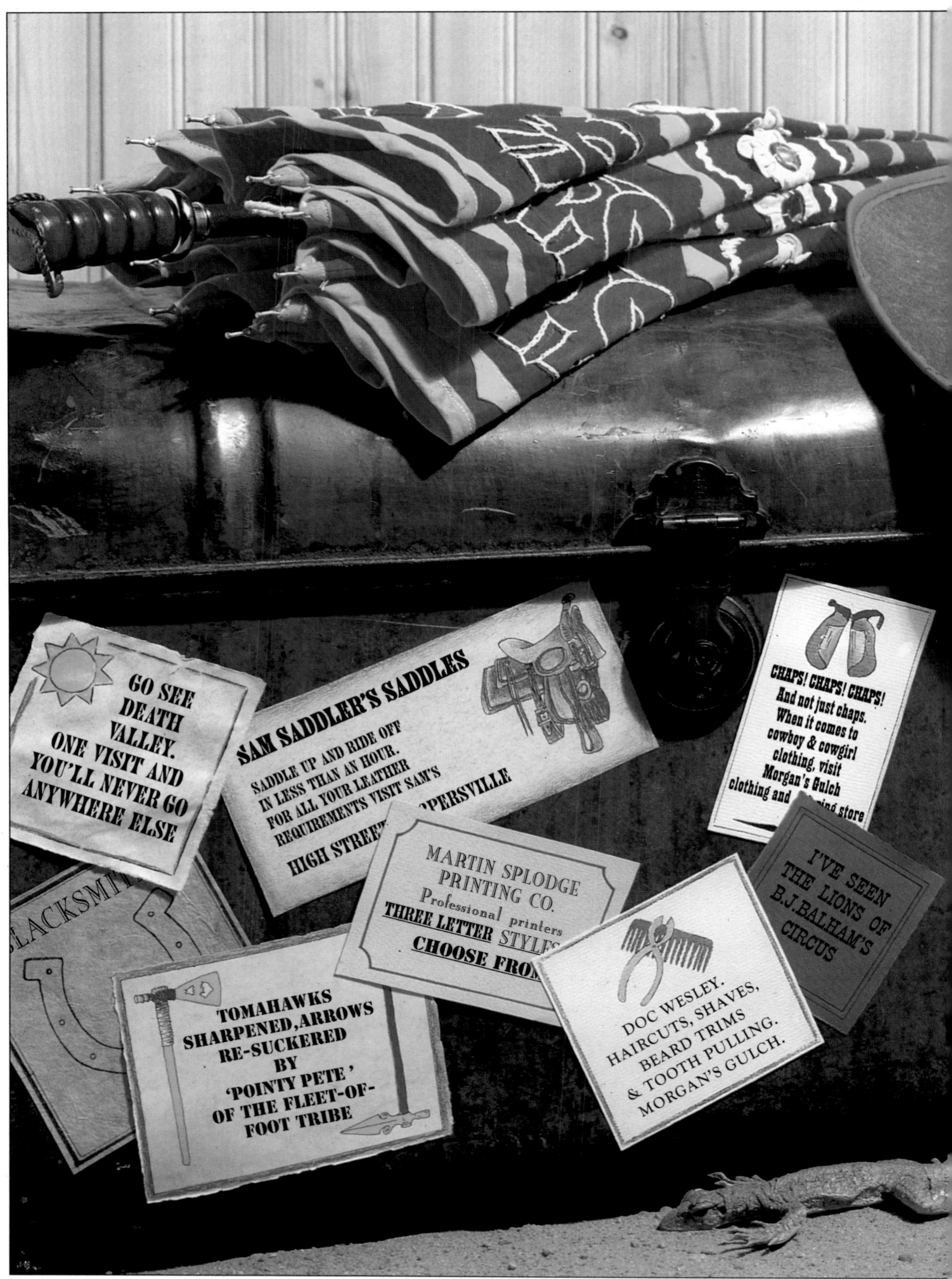
GO SEE DEATH VALLEY. ONE VISIT AND YOU'LL NEVER GO ANYWHERE ELSE
SAM SADDLER'S SADDLES
SADDLE UP AND RIDE OFF IN LESS THAN AN HOUR. FOR ALL YOUR LEATHER REQUIREMENTS VISIT SAM'S
HIGH STREE
OPERSVILLE
CHAPS! CHAPS! CHAPS! And not just chaps. When it comes to cowboy & cowgirl clothing, visit Morgan's Gulch clothing and
ing store
MARTIN SPLODGE PRINTING CO.
Professional printers
THREE LETTER STYLES
CHOOSE FROM
I'VE SEEN THE LIONS OF B.J.BALHAM'S CIRCUS
LACKSMIT
TOMAHAWKS SHARPENED,ARROWS RE-SUCKERED BY 'POINTY PETE' OF THE FLEET-OF-FOOT TRIBE
DOC WESLEY. HAIRCUTS, SHAVES, BEARD TRIMS & TOOTH PULLING. MORGAN'S GULCH.

STAGECOACH TO MORGAN'S GULCH

Time: Wednesday, 18th of August, 1891, 12:25pm
Place: Morgan's Gulch, Main Street, facing the sheriff's office

You arrive at the town of Morgan's Gulch on the noon stagecoach (which is late) and help the only other passenger, a preacher, down with his luggage. The place is dusty, that's for sure. Dusty and hot. It's time to check into your room.

Where are you staying? How do you get there?

This is to certify that
Clint & Betsy Gold of The Silver Dollar Saloon
are licensed, by law, to sell
OLDE SOCKS, DYN-O-MITE and
SCORPION'S TAIL
for one year, up until 31st of July, 1891
after which this permit must be renewed.
By order of Sheriff Goodhorn
Penalty for failing to renew: $2,00
DYN-O-MITE
THE TASTE OF STRAWBERRIES WITH THE KICK OF A MULE.
J.T.MONROE INDUSTRIES
SCORPION'S TAIL
Stingingly strong with a surprise in every bottle
OLDE SOCKS
THE INKY BLUE DRINK WITH A TANG OF STEWED CHEESE.
RAT POIS
KEEP LOCKED AWAY

THE SILVER DOLLAR SALOON

Time: Wednesday, 12:33pm
Place: In the bar of *The Silver Dollar Saloon*

You stride into the saloon where you'll be staying for the next few days. The piano player stops mid-tune. Up at the bar you order a Rattlesnake Shake. Clint, the landlord, glares at you. "Have you been sent to find out who shot the sheriff?" he asks. You nod. "We're better off without him," he says.

Why might Clint feel that?

JAILHOUSE BLUES

Time: Wednesday, 1:02pm
Place: Sheriff's office inside the jailhouse

With your luggage at the saloon, it's time to meet Deputy Williams. He isn't wearing a gun. "Sheriff's orders," he tells you, his feet up on the desk. "He's never let anybody carry a gun in this town." He points to a revolver. "He was shot with this one. The sheriff took it off Doc Wesley the day before he was shot, and left it on this here desk."

Doc Wesley? Who's he?

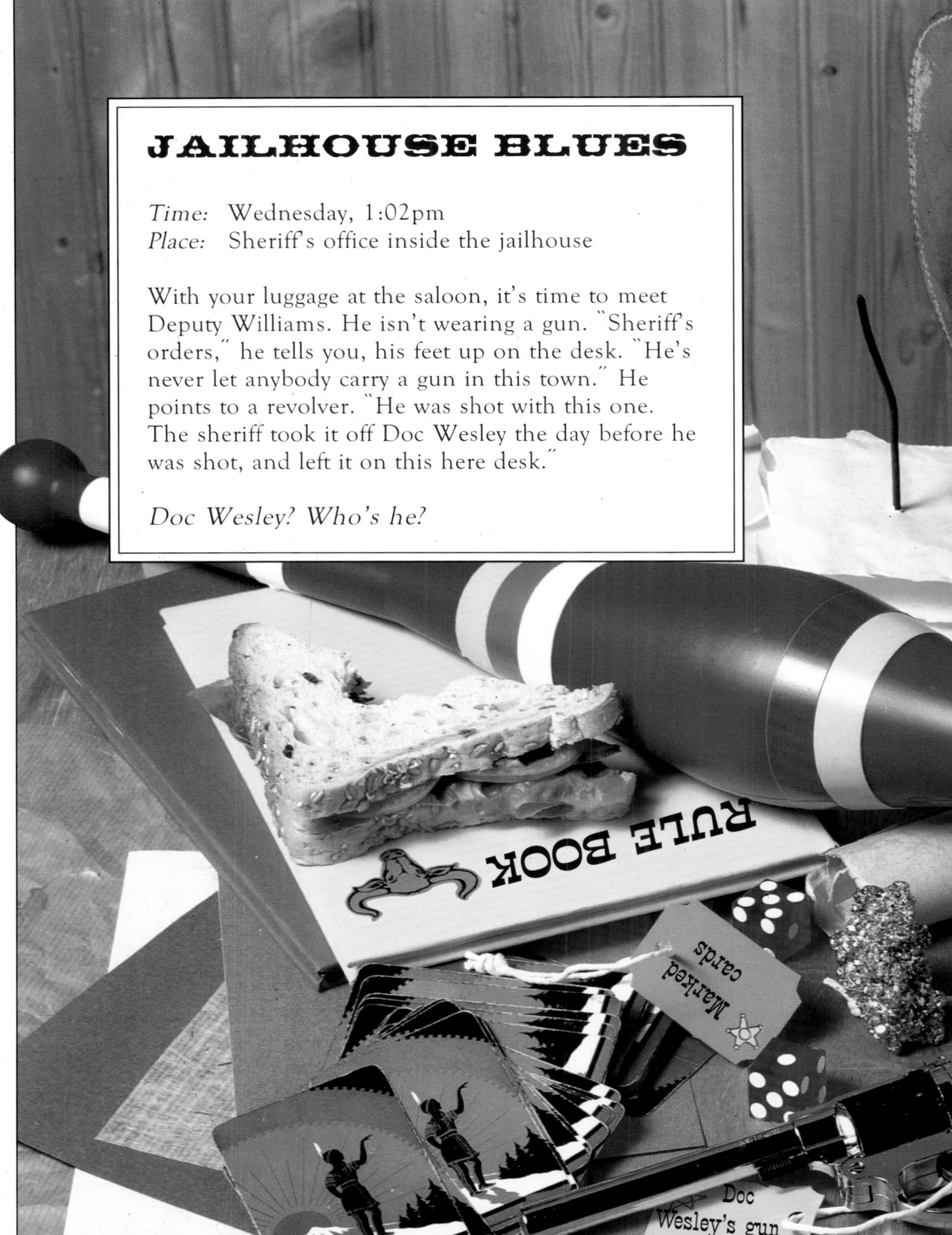

Fool's gold
Loaded dice
CONFISCATIONS BOOK
ARREST WARRANTS

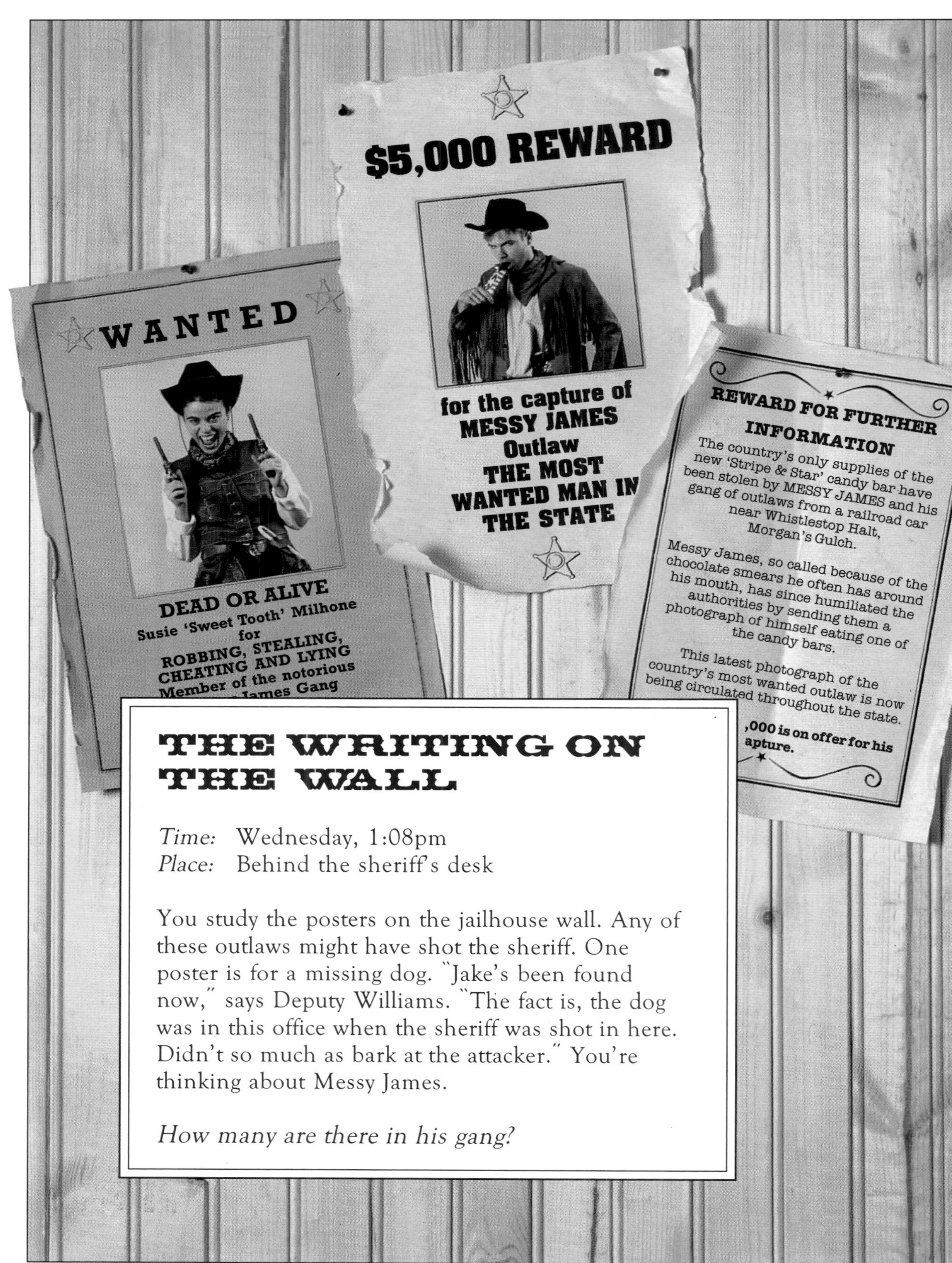

THE WRITING ON THE WALL

Time: Wednesday, 1:08pm
Place: Behind the sheriff's desk

You study the posters on the jailhouse wall. Any of these outlaws might have shot the sheriff. One poster is for a missing dog. "Jake's been found now," says Deputy Williams. "The fact is, the dog was in this office when the sheriff was shot in here. Didn't so much as bark at the attacker." You're thinking about Messy James.

How many are there in his gang?

A MESSAGE FROM STATE GOVERNOR HANK STICKLEBACK TO THE TOWNSFOLK OF MORGAN'S GULCH.
I would like to thank all you good people who did so much to try to capture Messy James & his evil gang of twelve following the robbery of the train near Whistlestop Halt.
Special thanks must go to Mort Grimcheek who lost his eye when attempting to topple James from his horse, and to Alf Cauldwell who lost his handkerchief.
May you wear your eyepatch with pride, Mr. Grimcheek. May you have a new handkerchief soon, Mr. Cauldwell.
Rest assured. These villains will be captured.
Hank Stickleback
HAVE YOU SEEN ANY OF THE FOLLOWING:
A one-armed woman calling herself 'Annie Thompkins'?
A man with a v-shaped scar on his right cheek, believed to be a retired & reformed member of the MESSY JAMES GANG.
A 6ft 7in bearded man with huge feet, wanted in connection with unpaid food bills.
IF SO, PLEASE INFORM YOUR LOCAL SHERIFF'S OFFICE AT ONCE.
WANTED
JAKE THE DOG
Has been missing for a week. Much missed by owner, Miss Jillian McGilligan of the Silver Dollar Saloon. An important part of her animal juggling act.
REWARD
'BABY-FACE' BODKIN
WANTED FOR QUESTIONING
$100 REWARD
Looks cute but isn't.
Explosives expert for MESSY JAMES GANG.
Always wears floral patterned shirts.

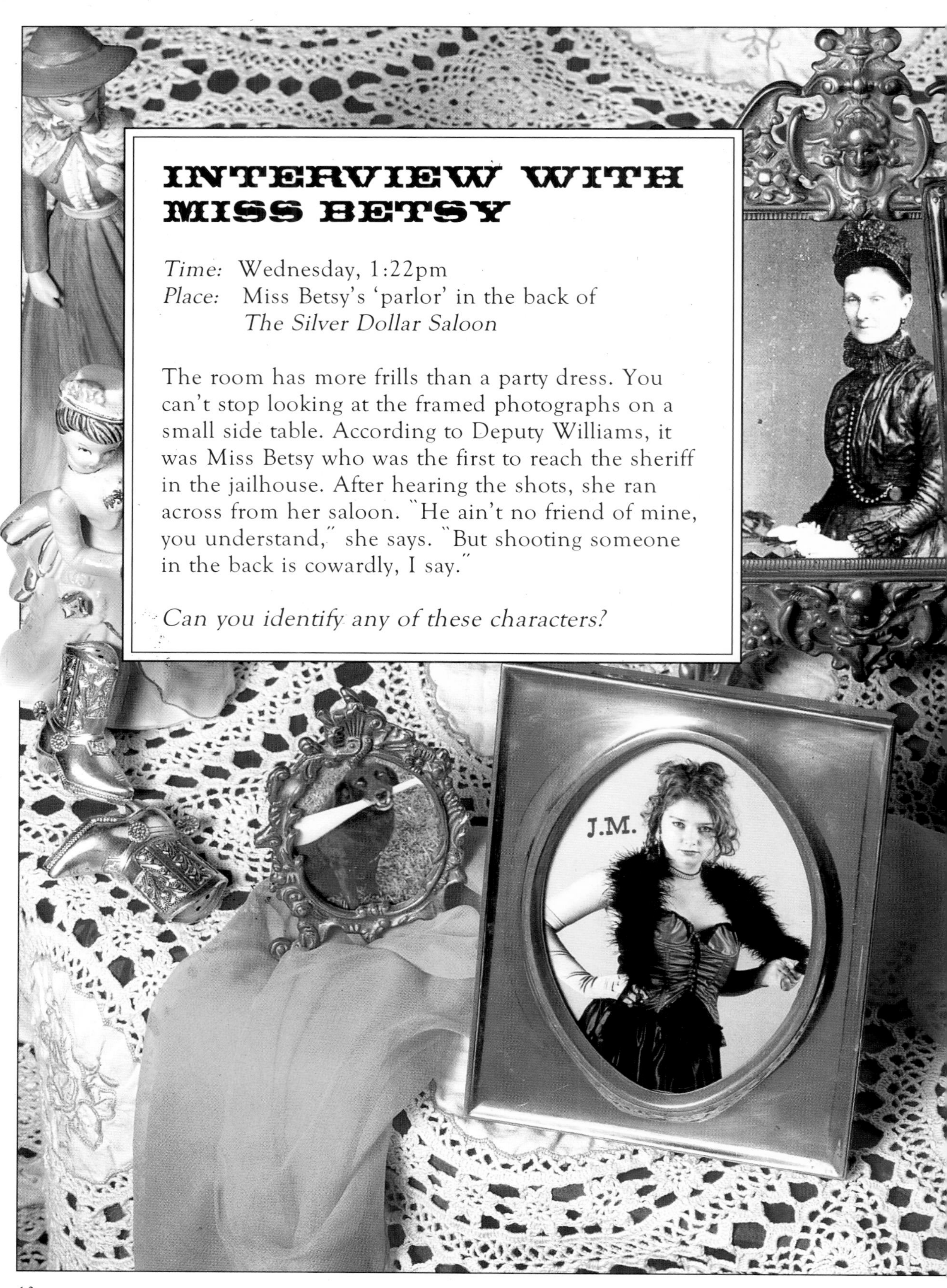

INTERVIEW WITH MISS BETSY

Time: Wednesday, 1:22pm
Place: Miss Betsy's 'parlor' in the back of *The Silver Dollar Saloon*

The room has more frills than a party dress. You can't stop looking at the framed photographs on a small side table. According to Deputy Williams, it was Miss Betsy who was the first to reach the sheriff in the jailhouse. After hearing the shots, she ran across from her saloon. "He ain't no friend of mine, you understand," she says. "But shooting someone in the back is cowardly, I say."

Can you identify any of these characters?

To Miss Betsy
With Best
Wishes
Doc Wesley

A HALF DOLLAR HAIRCUT

Time: Wednesday, 3:15pm
Place: Doc Wesley's tooth pulling and barbershop

It's time to speak to the man whose revolver was used to shoot the sheriff. You sit in Doc Wesley's barber's chair and stare into his wall cabinet. "Goodhorn took the gun off me the day before the shootin'," says the Doc. "Okay, so it has a hair trigger and sometimes goes off by accident when you pick it up . . . but the sheriff had no right to take it. He's never liked me seeing as how I'm new to these parts."

Interesting. How long has he had this shop?

TOOTH ACHE
MIXTURE
LOTION
SHANE
MARLDON
Town Tailor to
Morgan's Gulch
since 1882
FREE
FREE
FREE
MUSTACHE TRIM
DOC WESLEY
Hairdresser & Toothpuller
in Morgan's Gulch since 1890
FOR BEAUTIFUL
HAIR WEAR A
WILLIAMS WIG
LONDI'S
GINGER
BEER

AN ANONYMOUS TIP-OFF

Time: Wednesday, 7:08pm
Place: Your bedroom, *The Silver Dollar Saloon*

After a hard day of investigating, you're ready to read in bed. A message wrapped around a rock has just sailed through your bedroom window and landed on the quilt with a crash. It was lucky that the message didn't hit you on arrival, or you'd be in no fit state to read anything.

What does the message say?

OIOMOU OSOTOT OAOLOK OTOO OY
OOOUOA OBOOOU OTOTOH OEOSOH
OOOOOT OIONOG OOOFOS OHOEOR
OIOFOF OGOOOO ODOHOO ORONOT
OHOEOR OEOAOR OEOLOI OEOSOB
OEOION OGOSOP OROEOA ODOAOR
OOOUON ODOTOO OWONOA ONODOI
OWOAON OTOTOO OPOUOT OAOSOT
OOOPOT OOOTOH OEOMOM OEOEOT
OMOEOI ONOTOH OEOUON ODOEOR
OTOAOK OEOROS OAOTOE OLOEOV
OEONOO OCOLOO OCOKOC OOOMOE
OAOLOO ONOEII
'S GULCH NEWS
TROUBLE BREWING IN ELBOW CREEK
from our troublesome correspondent
There's nothing like a touch of gold fever to cause disputes, disagreements and fistfights over who owns what land. That's exactly what's happened in Elbow Creek since the discovery of gold in Elbow River.
"By rights that land belongs to the Fleet-of-Foot tribe," says Sheriff Goodhorn of Morgan's Gulch, "but there are some bad folks who claim otherwise."
Tomorrow's Morgan's Gulch News will carry a full report.
MISS ALICIA MONROE RETURNS TO COUNTY
from our social scene editor
Miss Alicia Monroe, beautiful daughter of Beef Baron and cattle king J.T. Monroe, has returned to live at the family homestead.

TO THE UNDERTAKER'S

Time: Wednesday, 11:07pm
Place: Carpentry room, the Undertaker's

Following the instructions in the message, you find yourself in a room of half-made coffins. You catch sight of a man in the shadows. "I'm Mort Grimcheek," he whispers. "Whatever you've heard, I didn't shoot the sheriff. The talk is that I want more guns around because more guns mean more deaths, an' more deaths mean more business for me. But it ain't true." There's something not quite right about the undertaker.

What is it?

IMPRESSIONS

Time: Wednesday, 11:14pm
Place: Outside the Undertaker's

You follow the fake Mort Grimcheek outside but he's up on his horse and away before you can shout 'imposter!' A huge lizard lumbers past. From the light of a window above, you search the ground for clues . . . a footprint . . . hoof prints . . . *anything* that might confirm who the man in the shadows really was. The candy bar wrapper's a giveaway.

Why?

ON THE TRACK

Time: Thursday, 10:26am
Place: On a steam train bound for *Whistlestop Halt*

A sunny morning. The girl in the train seat opposite you has her face half-hidden by a fan. She looks nervous. Following a lead, you're told that the real Mort Grimcheek is out of town . . . and that someone who really *hates* the sheriff is Jonah Johnson. You're on your way to visit him along the stretch of the Elbow River where he pans for gold. You look back at the girl.

Any clues as to who she could be?

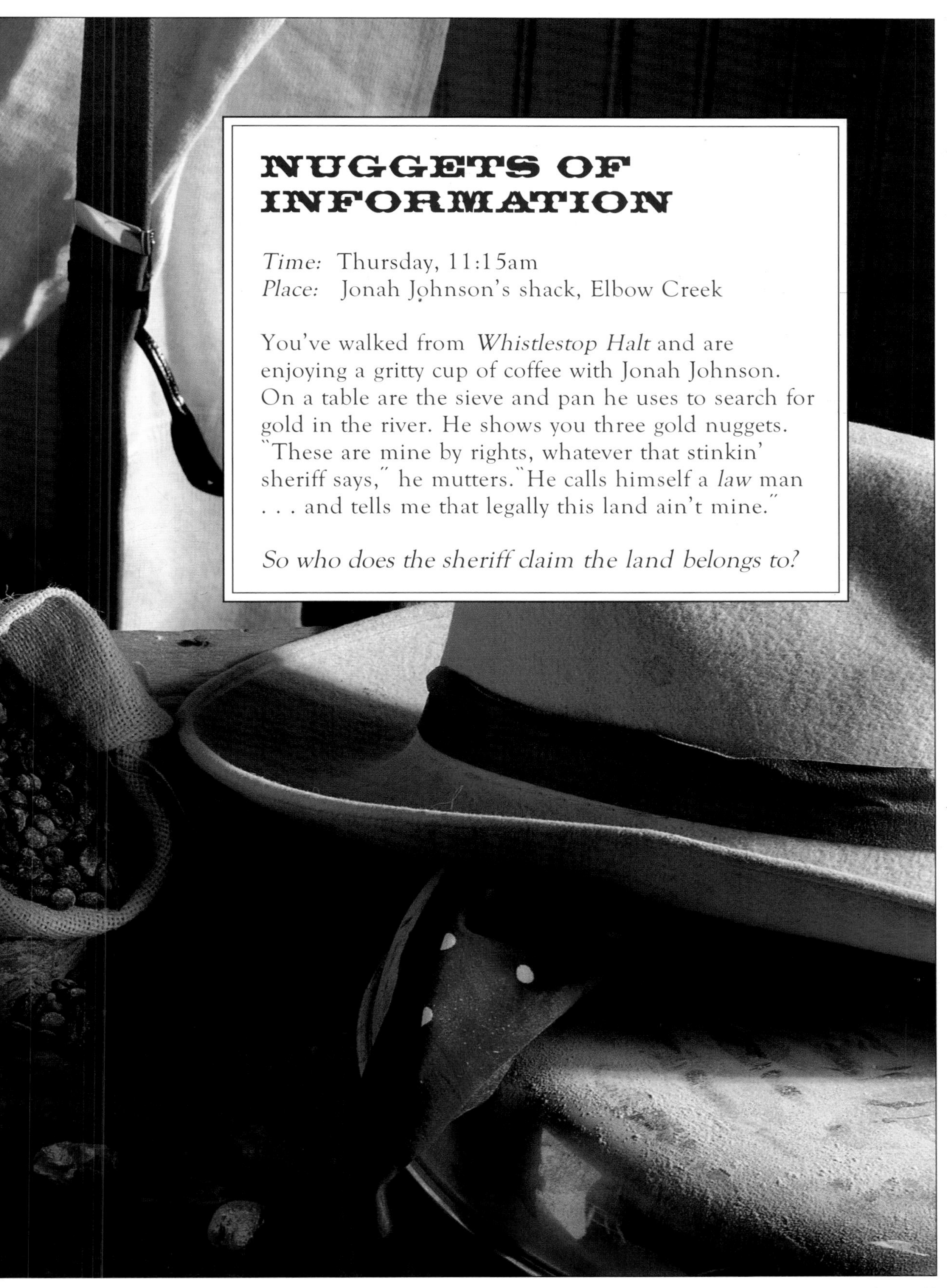

NUGGETS OF INFORMATION

Time: Thursday, 11:15am
Place: Jonah Johnson's shack, Elbow Creek

You've walked from *Whistlestop Halt* and are enjoying a gritty cup of coffee with Jonah Johnson. On a table are the sieve and pan he uses to search for gold in the river. He shows you three gold nuggets. "These are mine by rights, whatever that stinkin' sheriff says," he mutters. "He calls himself a *law* man . . . and tells me that legally this land ain't mine."

So who does the sheriff claim the land belongs to?

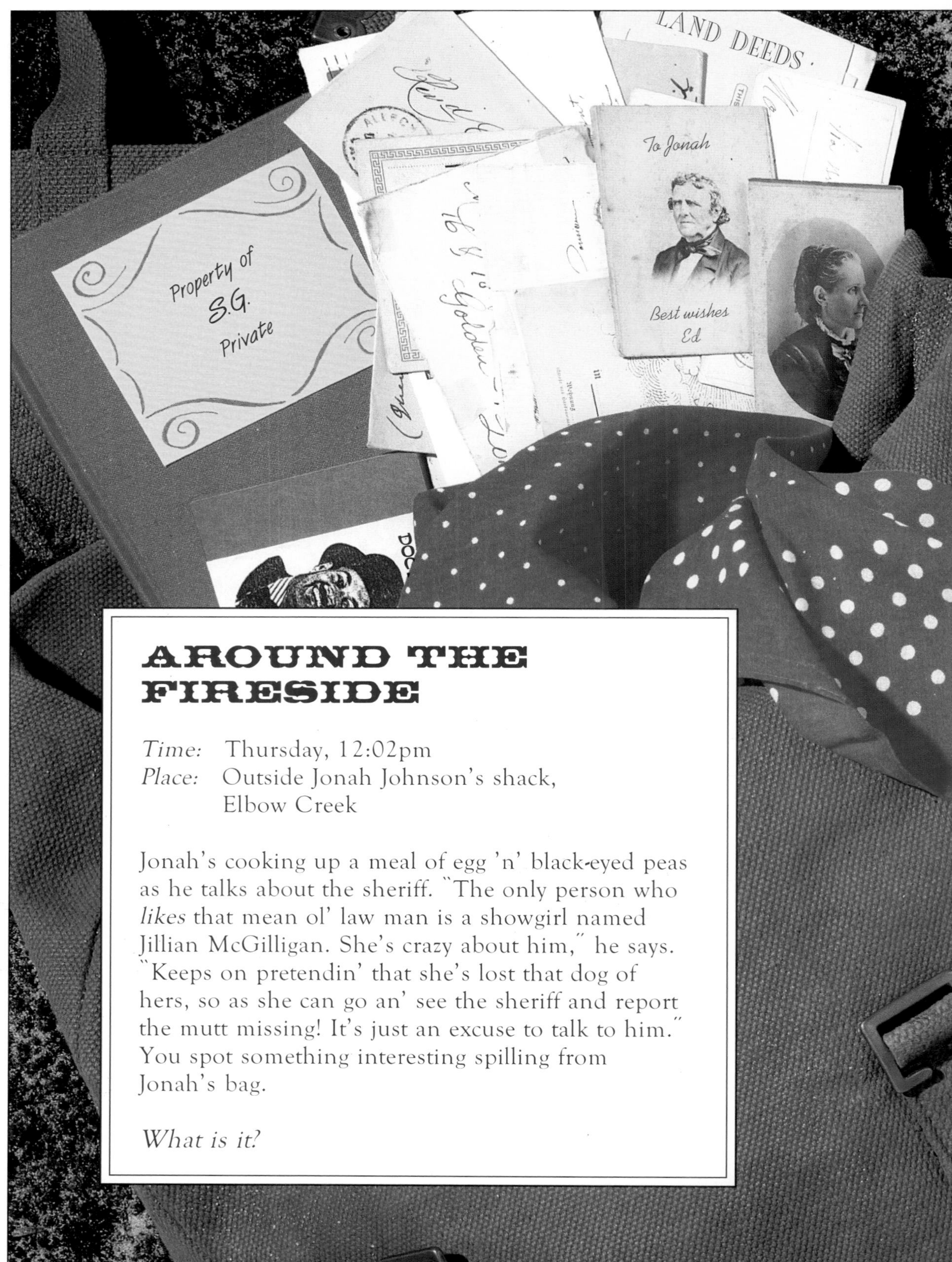

AROUND THE FIRESIDE

Time: Thursday, 12:02pm
Place: Outside Jonah Johnson's shack, Elbow Creek

Jonah's cooking up a meal of egg 'n' black-eyed peas as he talks about the sheriff. "The only person who *likes* that mean ol' law man is a showgirl named Jillian McGilligan. She's crazy about him," he says. "Keeps on pretendin' that she's lost that dog of hers, so as she can go an' see the sheriff and report the mutt missing! It's just an excuse to talk to him." You spot something interesting spilling from Jonah's bag.

What is it?

Old Timer's
BLACK-EYED
PEAS

The people of Morgan's Gulch are becoming more lawless by the day. No wonder that gutless Sheriff Meacher upped and left the town a year ago, leaving me the silver star of office and the job of upholding law and order.

Last Wednesday, I saw Max Henkle leave the general store and drop a piece of twine on the ground.

When I threatened him with a dollar fine for such disgraceful littering, he said 'Sorry' as though that would make things better. This sloppiness could lead to open rebellion on the streets.

I need a firmer hand.

As for Deputy Williams, I reckon he's after my job. Fat chance. He's more interested in his good looks than he is in keeping the bad element out of Morgan's Gulch – always admiring himself in the mirror and combing back his hair.

He spends more time in the barber's chair than he does behind his desk.

And as for all those quack doctors and medicine men, they're banned from Morgan's Gulch. I won't have a single one of them selling pills and potions in my town. No, sir.

BY THE BOOK

Time: Thursday, 12:35pm, after lunch
Place: Still outside Jonah's shack

Jonah is quick to point out that he'd simply *found* the sheriff's notebook. "I didn't wound him and take it off of him," he insists. "He must've dropped it." You flick through the pages and soon see why Sheriff Goodhorn is such an unpopular man in and around the town of Morgan's Gulch. He's a stickler for every rule and regulation. "Even the town tailor don't like 'im," grins Jonah. "And *he's* friends with just about everyone."

Who is the tailor? What's he done wrong?

Fines still to be paid:

MA GRIFFIN .....
for failing to wear her false teeth in a public place $3.00

LOU MACFARLANE .....
for failing to raise his hat to Miss Betsy on Sunday $1.50

DIRK MULGREW .....
Speaking with his mouth full 50c

BIG BAD WITHERS .....
Sneezing without a handkerchief in the bar $2.00

HANE MARLDON .....
chewing gum on a Friday $3.00

NNY NORTON .....
dercharging senior citizens 50c

WAITING IN A TEEPEE

Time: Thursday, 2:45pm
Place: Inside a teepee of the Fleet-of-Foot tribe

You sit staring at the rug-covered floor, waiting to see if Chief Peacemaker will agree to talk to you. You found his name in the sheriff's notebook and borrowed Jonah's mule to ride out here to the tribe's settlement. Something catches your eye that suggests that the chief's braves are doing more in Elbow River than just hunting and fishing.

What is it?

A POWWOW WITH THE CHIEF

Time: Thursday, 3:15pm
Place: Chief Peacemaker's teepee

From the way they treat his picture, you reckon that Sheriff Goodhorn isn't too popular around these parts. But did one of the Fleet-of-Foot's braves actually shoot him? "Goodhorn does not like people carrying guns and neither do I," says Chief Peacemaker. "My braves have no interest in white men's weapons," he says. "We hunt with spears and arrows."

Do you believe him?

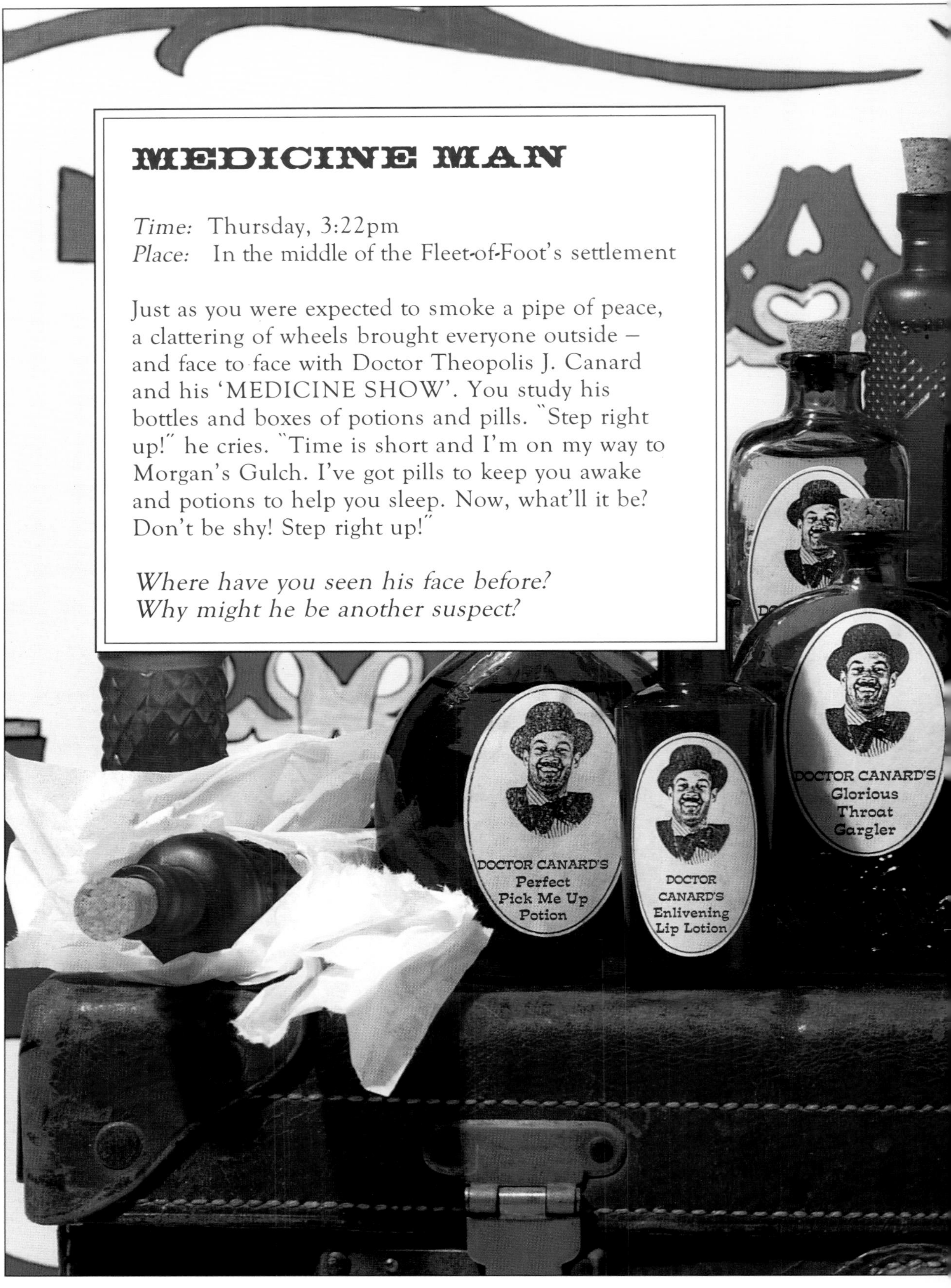

Time: Thursday, 3:22pm
Place: In the middle of the Fleet-of-Foot's settlement

Just as you were expected to smoke a pipe of peace, a clattering of wheels brought everyone outside – and face to face with Doctor Theopolis J. Canard and his 'MEDICINE SHOW'. You study his bottles and boxes of potions and pills. "Step right up!" he cries. "Time is short and I'm on my way to Morgan's Gulch. I've got pills to keep you awake and potions to help you sleep. Now, what'll it be? Don't be shy! Step right up!"

Where have you seen his face before?
Why might he be another suspect?

DOCTOR CANARD'S
Amazing
Wrinkle
Remover
DOCTOR CANARD'S
Fantastic
Foot Swamp
Soother
DOCTOR CANARD'S
Tested
Tiredness
Tablets
DOCTOR CANARD'S
Hearty
Headache
Healers
DOCTOR CANARD'S
Comfy Kidney
Pills
Take two daily

Wednesday.
Don't forget to visit C.P. about
possibility of purchases.
J. T. MONROE INDUSTRIES
Founder & President J.T. Monroe
Offices worldwide.
Order more
DYN-O-MITE
Hank Stickleback
Hank Stickleback
State Governor

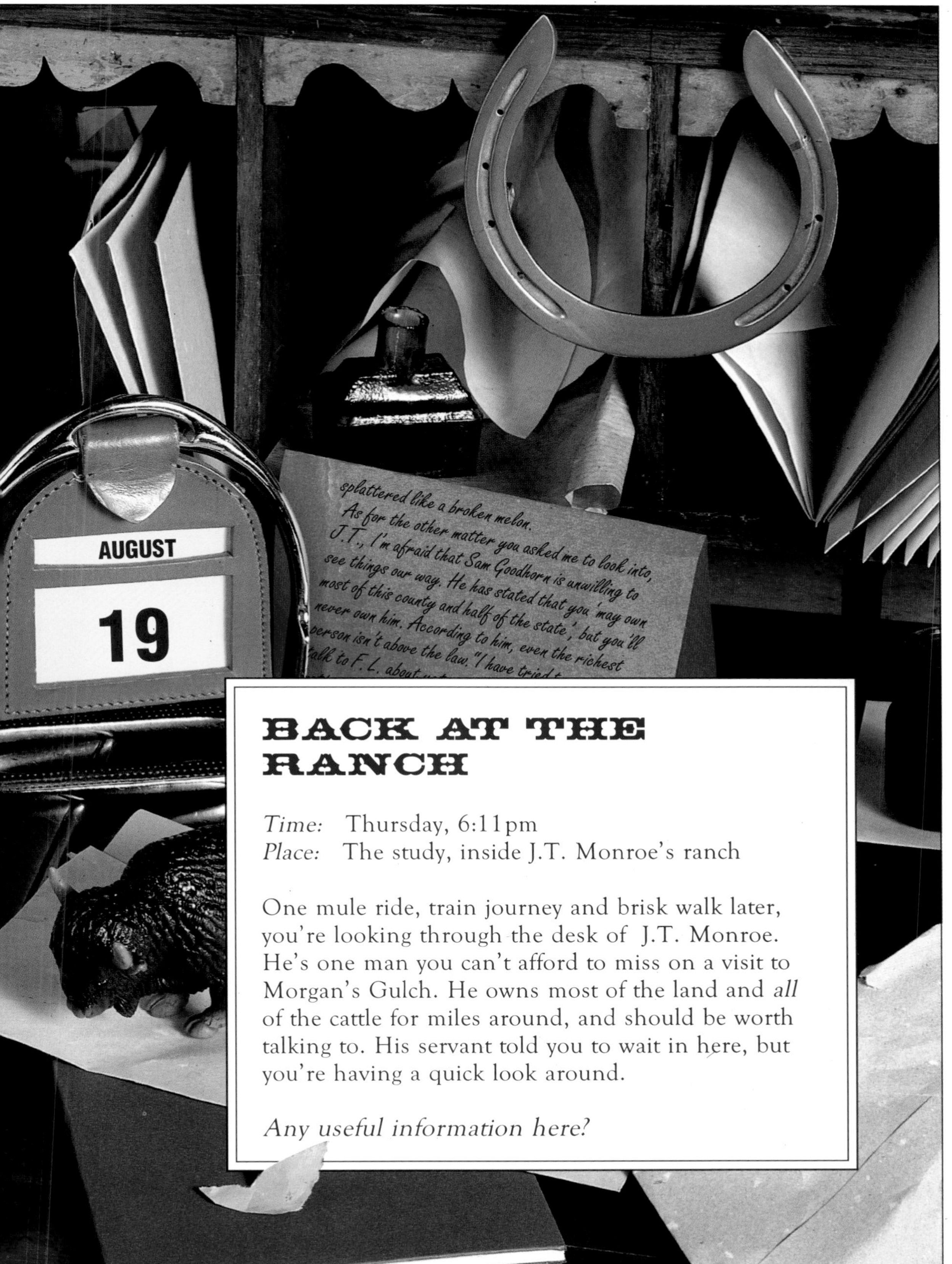

BACK AT THE RANCH

Time: Thursday, 6:11pm
Place: The study, inside J.T. Monroe's ranch

One mule ride, train journey and brisk walk later, you're looking through the desk of J.T. Monroe. He's one man you can't afford to miss on a visit to Morgan's Gulch. He owns most of the land and *all* of the cattle for miles around, and should be worth talking to. His servant told you to wait in here, but you're having a quick look around.

Any useful information here?

THE CATTLE KING

Time: Thursday, 7:00pm on the dot
Place: J.T. Monroe's stables

You're finally taken out to meet the great man. He doesn't look like a millionaire. He looks more like a cowboy, from the Stetson on his head down to those cowboy boots of his you're admiring. "Sheriff Goodhorn's a little law man who's too big for his britches," says J.T. "But I didn't have him shot." Local talk, however, is that J.T. is selling guns to the Fleet-of-Foot tribe.

Any clues that he's been to see them?

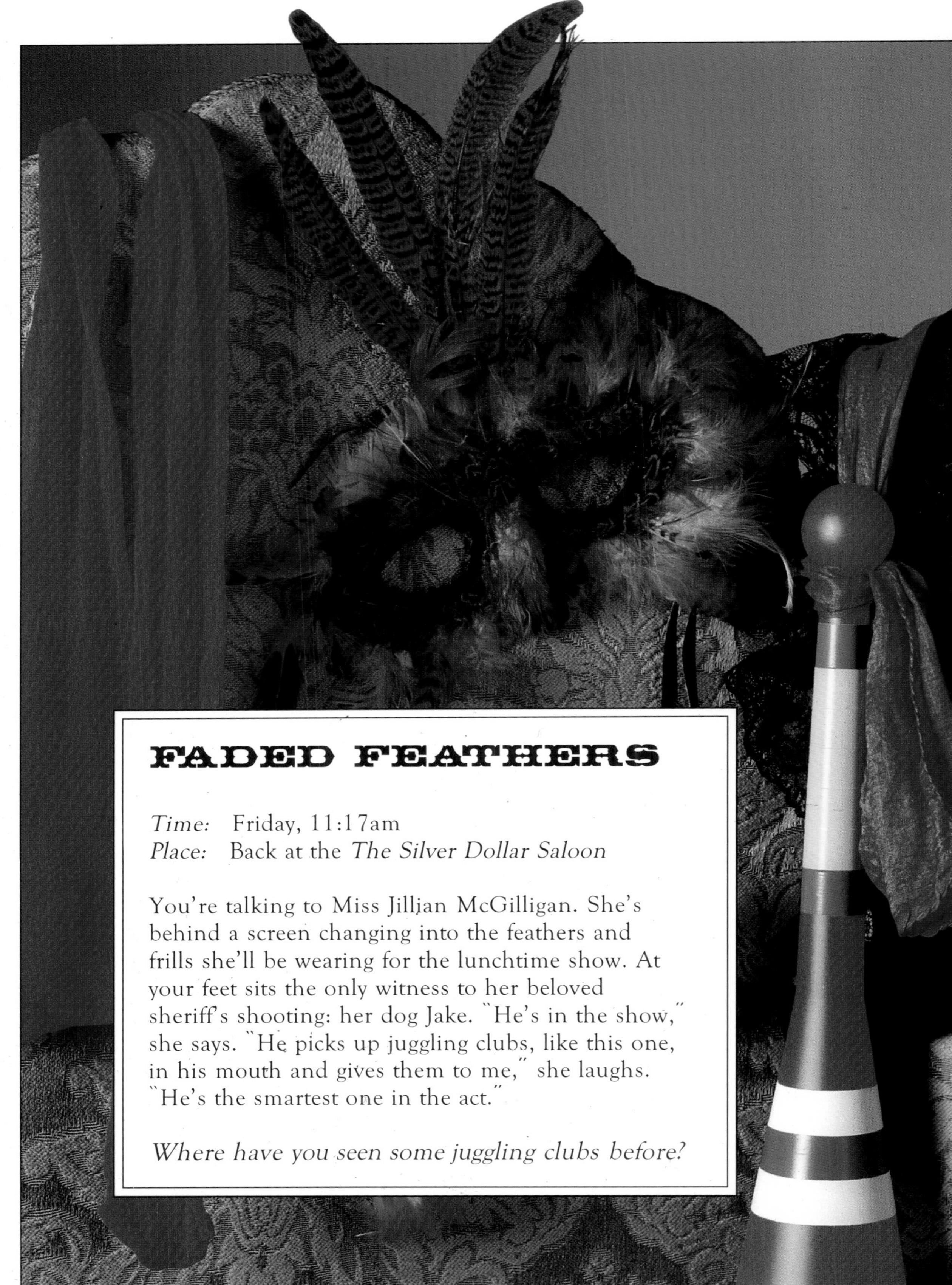

FADED FEATHERS

Time: Friday, 11:17am
Place: Back at the *The Silver Dollar Saloon*

You're talking to Miss Jillian McGilligan. She's behind a screen changing into the feathers and frills she'll be wearing for the lunchtime show. At your feet sits the only witness to her beloved sheriff's shooting: her dog Jake. "He's in the show," she says. "He picks up juggling clubs, like this one, in his mouth and gives them to me," she laughs. "He's the smartest one in the act."

Where have you seen some juggling clubs before?

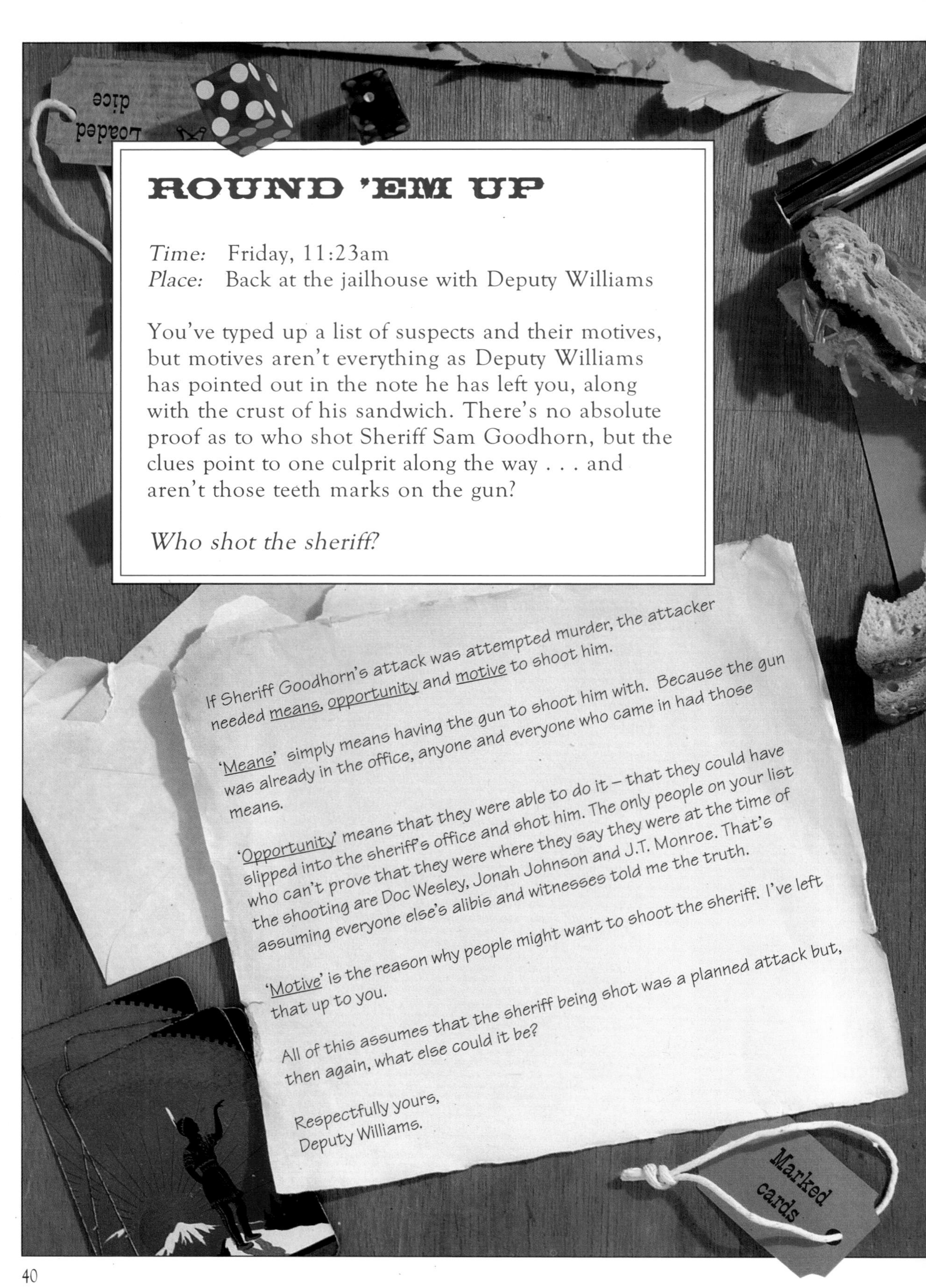

ROUND 'EM UP

Time: Friday, 11:23am
Place: Back at the jailhouse with Deputy Williams

You've typed up a list of suspects and their motives, but motives aren't everything as Deputy Williams has pointed out in the note he has left you, along with the crust of his sandwich. There's no absolute proof as to who shot Sheriff Sam Goodhorn, but the clues point to one culprit along the way . . . and aren't those teeth marks on the gun?

Who shot the sheriff?

If Sheriff Goodhorn's attack was attempted murder, the attacker needed means, opportunity and motive to shoot him.

'Means' simply means having the gun to shoot him with. Because the gun was already in the office, anyone and everyone who came in had those means.

'Opportunity' means that they were able to do it – that they could have slipped into the sheriff's office and shot him. The only people on your list who can't prove that they were where they say they were at the time of the shooting are Doc Wesley, Jonah Johnson and J.T. Monroe. That's assuming everyone else's alibis and witnesses told me the truth.

'Motive' is the reason why people might want to shoot the sheriff. I've left that up to you.

All of this assumes that the sheriff being shot was a planned attack but, then again, what else could it be?

Respectfully yours,
Deputy Williams.

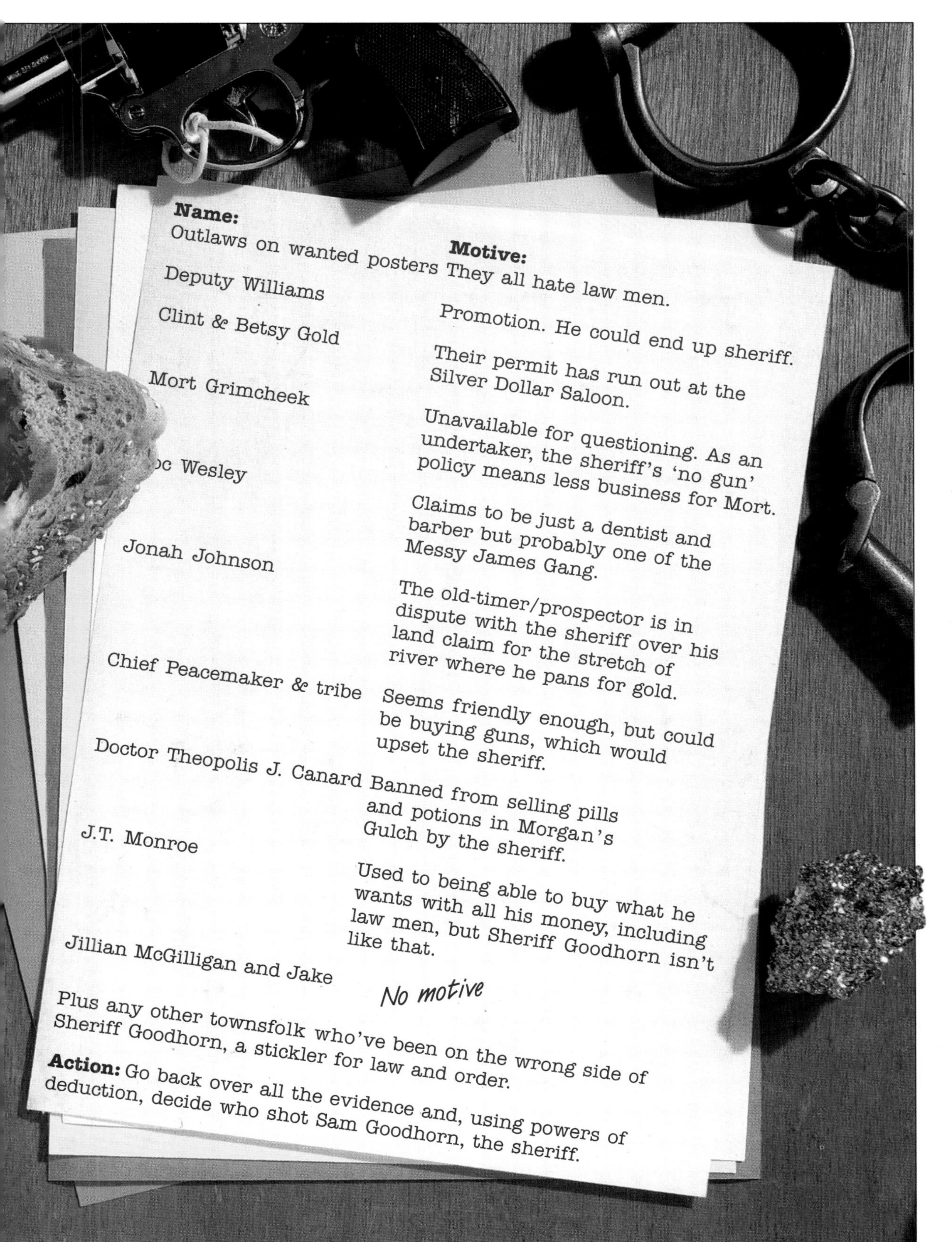
Name:
Motive:
Outlaws on wanted posters They all hate law men.
Deputy Williams
Promotion. He could end up sheriff.
Clint & Betsy Gold
Their permit has run out at the Silver Dollar Saloon.
Mort Grimcheek
Unavailable for questioning. As an undertaker, the sheriff's 'no gun' policy means less business for Mort.
oc Wesley
Claims to be just a dentist and barber but probably one of the Messy James Gang.
Jonah Johnson
The old-timer/prospector is in dispute with the sheriff over his land claim for the stretch of river where he pans for gold.
Chief Peacemaker & tribe Seems friendly enough, but could be buying guns, which would upset the sheriff.
Doctor Theopolis J. Canard Banned from selling pills and potions in Morgan's Gulch by the sheriff.
J.T. Monroe
Used to being able to buy what he wants with all his money, including law men, but Sheriff Goodhorn isn't like that.
Jillian McGilligan and Jake
No motive
Plus any other townsfolk who've been on the wrong side of Sheriff Goodhorn, a stickler for law and order.
Action: Go back over all the evidence and, using powers of deduction, decide who shot Sam Goodhorn, the sheriff.

HELPFUL HINTS

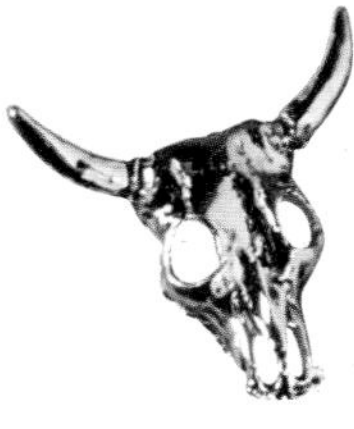

PAGES 2 & 3
Hank Stickleback can help you here.

PAGES 4 & 5
It's the sheriff's duty to make sure that everything is up to date.

PAGES 6 & 7
The answer lies on someone's luggage.

PAGES 8 & 9
The answer's in the small print. Read it carefully.

PAGES 10 & 11
The posters on the sheriff's wall should help you identify *three* characters.

PAGES 12 & 13
His card says he's been in Morgan's Gulch 'since 1890'. What year is this investigation taking place?

PAGES 14 & 15
Oooo? I don't think they're all necessary.

PAGES 16 & 17
Isn't there something about Mort on the sheriff's office wall? There are some pictures of some very nasty characters there too.

PAGES 18 & 19
The candy should wrap this riddle up.

PAGES 20 & 21
Perhaps she's been mentioned in the newspapers.

PAGES 22 & 23
Look at your bedtime reading matter again.

PAGES 24 & 25
It belongs to the sheriff.

PAGES 26 & 27
The tailor has been named somewhere before. Match this name with one of the names here.

PAGES 28 & 29
There's an object here similar to something Jonah Johnson has back in his hut.

PAGES 30 & 31
The answer lies in the other teepee.

PAGES 32 & 33
Is he a friend of Miss Betsy's? And doesn't Jonah take his pills? As for why he might be a suspect, what does the sheriff have to say about quack doctors?

PAGES 34 & 35
Something on J.T.Monroe's desk is revealing about his attitude to lawmen.

PAGES 36 & 37
A boot could hold a clue . . . or not.

PAGES 38 & 39
You've seen two. One in black and white, and one very near the beginning of your investigation.

PAGES 40 & 41
Go back over all the evidence . . .

ANSWERS

PAGES 2 & 3

According to Governor Hank Stickleback's letter on page 1, he's booked you a room at the *Silver Dollar Saloon* – so that's where you should be going next. You can find out where it is in **Main Street** by studying the map he gave you.

PAGES 4 & 5

On the bar are bottles of **DYN-O-MITE**, **SCORPION'S TAIL** and **OLDE SOCKS**. According to the permit behind Clint's shoulder, these can't be sold without an up-to-date permit. This one ran out on 31st of July, 1891 . . . and Hank Stickleback didn't send you his letter until August. With the sheriff out of the way, it looks as if Clint hasn't bothered to buy a new permit. He can sell the drinks illegally.

PAGES 6 & 7

Doc Wesley's name appears on one of the labels on the preacher's trunk that you helped to get down from the stagecoach on pages 2 & 3. It says that he does 'HAIRCUTS, SHAVES, BEARD TRIMMING AND TOOTH PULLING' in Morgan's Gulch. That makes him the local barber and tooth-puller . . . not the most popular job in town!

PAGES 8 & 9

According to the poster headed '*A MESSAGE FROM STATE GOVERNOR . . .*', Messy James and '*his evil gang of twelve*' were involved in a recent robbery . . . so there are thirteen of them, including Messy himself!

PAGES 10 & 11

There are three 'familiar' characters who can be identified in Miss Betsy's photographs. The most obvious is probably Doc Wesley. He's signed his photo . . . but there's something else about him that could be important. According to the '**HAVE YOU SEEN**' poster on pages 8 & 9, the hunt is on for '**A man with a v-shaped scar on his right cheek, believed to be a retired & reformed member of the Messy James gang**'. Doesn't he have such a scar?

Jake the dog is also easy to spot. There's another picture of him on a **WANTED** poster on the jailhouse wall on pages 8 & 9. In the description, he's described as being part of Miss Jillian McGilligan's '**animal juggling act**'.

The woman in the photo next to Jake is dressed as a showgirl and has the initials **J.M.** on her photo. It's more than likely, then, that's she's Jake's owner, Miss Jillian McGilligan '**of the Silver Dollar Saloon**' .

PAGES 12 & 13

According to Doc Wesley's card, on the righthand door of his cabinet, he's been 'Hairdresser & Toothpuller in Morgan's Gulch since 1890'. According to the date on Hank Stickleback's letter (and the date under 'Time' on pages 2 & 3), it's now August 1891. That means that the Doc's been in business here from anything between 9 months and almost 18 months. This could tie in with him being a recently retired outlaw.

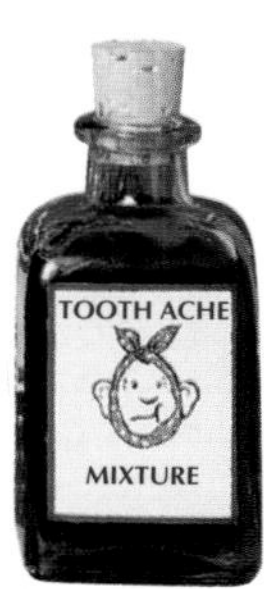

PAGES 14 & 15

The message tied to the rock thrown through your bedroom window may look like it's in a difficult code, but it's easy to read once you've cracked it. There's a letter 'o' in front of each and every letter. All the letters have been divided into groups of six. Simply remove the extra'o's, divide the remaining letters into words, add punctuation and the message reads:

I MUST TALK TO YOU ABOUT THE SHOOTING OF SHERIFF GOODHORN THERE ARE LIES BEING SPREAD AROUND TOWN AND I WANT TO PUT A STOP TO THEM. MEET ME IN THE UNDERTAKERS AT ELEVEN O' CLOCK. COME ALONE!!

PAGES 16 & 17

The real Mort Grimcheek, undertaker, wears an eyepatch. In the '*MESSAGE TO THE PEOPLE OF MORGAN'S GULCH*' on pages 8 & 9, the State Governor gives special praise to Mr. Grimcheek for losing his eye '*when attempting to topple James from his horse*'. This man has two eyes . . . and looks suspiciously like Messy James, photographed on the wanted poster in the sheriff's office.

PAGES 18 & 19

The dropped wrapper looks like the 'Stripe & Star' candy bar being held by Messy James in the poster on page 8. According to that poster **'the country's only supplies of the new 'Stripe & Star' candy bar have been stolen by MESSY JAMES and his gang.'** This further adds to the evidence that the man you've been talking to is Messy James himself.

PAGES 20 & 21

An article in **MORGAN'S GULCH NEWS**, in your room at the Silver Dollar Saloon on pages 14 &15, describes J.T. Monroe's daughter, Alicia, as being 'instantly recognizable with a beauty spot on her cheek and a bull's skull ring on her finger.' The woman opposite you on the train has both the beauty spot and the ring. It's therefore likely that she's Miss Alicia Monroe.

PAGES 22 & 23

The answer once again lies in the newspaper on pages 14 & 15, but in a different article. Under the heading **'TROUBLE BREWING IN ELBOW CREEK'**, the sheriff is quoted as saying: 'By rights that land belongs to the Fleet-of-Foot tribe.'

PAGES 24 & 25

There seem to be a number of interesting items sticking out of the old-timer's bag, but the most curious must be the book marked '*Property of S. G. Private.*' S. G. are Sheriff Sam Goodhorn's initials. This must be his book.

PAGES 26 & 27

The first step is to work out who the tailor is. For this you'll need to go back and look at the cards in Doc Wesley's barbershop on pages 12 & 13. Sure enough, one of the advertisements reads: 'SHANE MARLDON Town Tailor to Morgan's Gulch.' Now all you have to do is find the name in the sheriff's notebook. Marldon's crime is spelled out as: '*chewing gum on a Friday*'.

PAGES 28 & 29

Among the jumble of bows, arrows, tomahawks and spears lies a sieve which is almost identical to the one you saw on the table in Jonah Johnson's shack on pages 22 & 23. Jonah said that he used *his* to search for gold in Elbow River. This means that it's likely that the Fleet-of-Foot tribe are using *theirs* for a similar purpose. They're doing a little gold prospecting of their own.

PAGES 30 & 31

Although Chief Peacemaker says that his braves only hunt with spears and arrows, there is a leaflet for the 'Sharpe-Shooter.45' lying, half-covered, in the teepee you just left on pages 28 & 29. Perhaps he is more interested in 'white men's weapons' than he is letting on.

Interestingly, in his letter to you on page 1, Hank Stickleback describes the revolver used to shoot the sheriff being made by the '*Sharpe Gun & Locksmith Company*'. The gun in the leaflet is also described as having a 'golden finish'. It seems likely that Doc Wesley's confiscated gun was, therefore, like the one in this leaflet: a Sharpe-Shooter .45.

PAGES 32 & 33

You've seen this face twice before. Once, on a packet of pills sticking out of the top of Jonah Johnson's bag when he was cooking up egg 'n' beans around the fire, on pages 24 & 25. Before that, in Miss Betsy's parlor on pages 10 & 11, there was a photograph of him raising his hat. Miss Betsy seems to have photos of plenty of strange characters . . .

And why might Doctor Canard have had reason to shoot the sheriff? In his notebook on pages 26 & 27, Sheriff Goodhorn wrote: '*As for all those quack doctors and medicine men, they're banned from Morgan's Gulch. I won't have a single one of them selling pills and potions in my town. No, sir.*' With the sheriff out of the way, Doctor Canard is now free to travel to the town. But would the doctor go so far as to shoot a person for that?

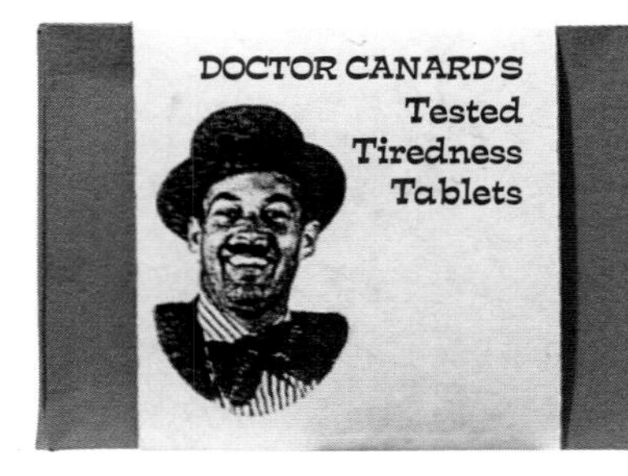

PAGES 34 & 35

There are a number of items that suggest J.T. Monroe might want the sheriff out of the way.

As his headed notepaper makes very clear, he is founder and president of J.T. MONROE INDUSTRIES. If you look at the label of the bottle of **DYN-O-MITE** on the bar on pages 4 & 5, you'll see that it's made by J.T. Monroe Industries . . . and if the Silver Dollar Saloon wasn't allowed to sell it any more because its permit has run out, J.T. would lose money.

Then there's the matter of the note on J.T's desk in which Sheriff Goodhorn is quotes as saying that J.T. '*may own most of this county and half of the state, but you'll never own [me]*.' J.T. is the kind of man who would far rather have a lawman he could bribe.

PAGES 36 & 37

J.T. is only wearing a spur on one boot. The other spur must have fallen off somewhere. It has, and you've seen it . . . in Chief Peacemaker's teepee on pages 30 & 31. Not only that, sticking out of one of the drawers of J.T's desk, on pages 34 & 35, is the note: 'Don't forget to visit C.P. about possibility of purchases'. 'C.P.' could stand for Chief Peacemaker, and there was also that Sharpe Gun & Locksmith leaflet in the Fleet-of-Foot's wigwam. It seems probable that this talk of J.T. selling guns to the tribe is true.

PAGES 38 & 39

There was a juggling club in the mouth of Jake the dog in the photograph on Miss Betsy's table on pages 10 & 11, which isn't surprising considering his role in Miss Jillian McGilligan's act at the *Silver Dollar Saloon*.

There was also a (blue) juggling club on the sheriff's desk on page 6. Perhaps Jake had this in his mouth when he was found and taken to the sheriff's office on the day that Sheriff Goodhorn was shot.

PAGES 40 & 41

So you want to know who shot the sheriff? Well, you won't find the answer on this page. This is your last chance to decide who *you* think did it. Remember those words of advice on page 1: 'you'll need to make your own deductions and use your best powers of reasoning. This is real detective work. You'll need to fill in the gaps.' Ready? Then turn the page and hold it up against a mirror.

The only living breathing creature known to be in the jailhouse with the sheriff at the time of the shooting was Jillian McGilligan's dog, Jake. According to Jonah Johnson on pages 24 & 25, Jillian "keeps on pretendin' that she's lost that dog of hers, just so as she can go and see the sheriff . . . She's crazy about him." Jake had been found and taken to the sheriff.

Jake likes holding things in his mouth. You can see him holding a juggling club in one of the photographs on Miss Betsy's table on pages 10 & 11. As Jillian McGilligan explained on pages 38 & 39, the dog was trained to pick up these juggling clubs in his mouth as a part of her performance. "He's the smartest one in the act," she said.

And what about the gun itself? A Sharpe .45, it belonged to Doc Wesley and was already on the sheriff's desk before the sheriff was shot. According to Deputy Willliams on pages 4 & 5 "Sheriff Goodhorn took it off Doc Wesley the day before" the shooting. On pages 12 & 13, Doc Wesley described the gun as having "a hair trigger and sometimes goes off by accident when you pick it up."

So let's look at the facts: the gun, that can go off by accident without the the trigger having to be pulled properly, is on a desk that also has a juggling club on it (see pages 6 & 7). The sheriff is shot in the lower back and in the hat that he's holding at his side . . . and the gun has teeth marks on its handle.

Jake the dog shot the sheriff. He had no idea what he was doing of course. He simply picked up the gun in his mouth (perhaps he was reaching for the blue juggling club) and it went off twice, shooting the poor old sheriff. No one is to blame. Except, perhaps, for Sheriff Goodhorn himself. He should have thought to take the bullets from the gun!
So the culprit was one of those shown on one of the wanted posters after all.

BY THE WAY . . .

Like any good detective, you're probably wondering why someone should pretend to be Mort Grimcheek the undertaker and act so suspiciously. The answer is simple. As you know, the man pretending to be Mort was none other than the outlaw Messy James himself. James was sure that he'd be Number One suspect for shooting the sheriff. By pretending to be Mort and protesting his innocence, he was actually trying to plant the idea in your mind that the undertaker had good reason for shooting Sheriff Goodhorn. It was a double bluff.

James picked on Mort Grimcheek to take the heat off himself, because Mort almost managed to capture him once. You can read about that in the poster on pages 8 & 9.

Reports have just come in that Sheriff Goodhorn is making a full recovery.

First published in 1996 by Usborne Publishing Limited, Usborne House, 83-85 Saffron Hill, London EC1N 8RT, England.
© Copyright 1996 Usborne Publishing Ltd.
The name Usborne and the device are Trade marks of Usborne Publishing Ltd. All rights reserved.
No part of this publication may be reproduced, stored in any retrieval system, or transmitted in any form or by any means, electronic, mechanical, photocopying, recording or otherwise, without the prior permission of the publisher.
Printed in Spain U.E. First published in America March 1997.